Sandy Creek
NEW YORK

An Imprint of Sterling Publishing
387 Park Avenue South
New York, NY 10016

Written by Annie Baker
Illustrated by Barroux
Edited by Laura Baker
Designed by Ailsa Cullen
Production by Jonathan Wakeham

ISBN 978-1-4351-4515-3

Printed in Heshan, China
Lot:10 9 8 7 6 5 4 3 2 1
11/2012

I LOVE YOU WHEN ...

Sandy Creek
NEW YORK

I love you when it's warm and sunny.

I love you when you're being funny.

I love you when it's wet outside.

I love you when you want to hide.

I love you when it's very breezy!

I even love you when you're sneezy.

I love you when we rush to and fro,

and I love you when there's nowhere to go.

I love you when you're sad and weepy.

when you wriggle ...

I love you when you're snuggly.

I love you when you're huggly.

I love you when you say, "I love you, too."

But mostly, I love you whenever
I'm with you.

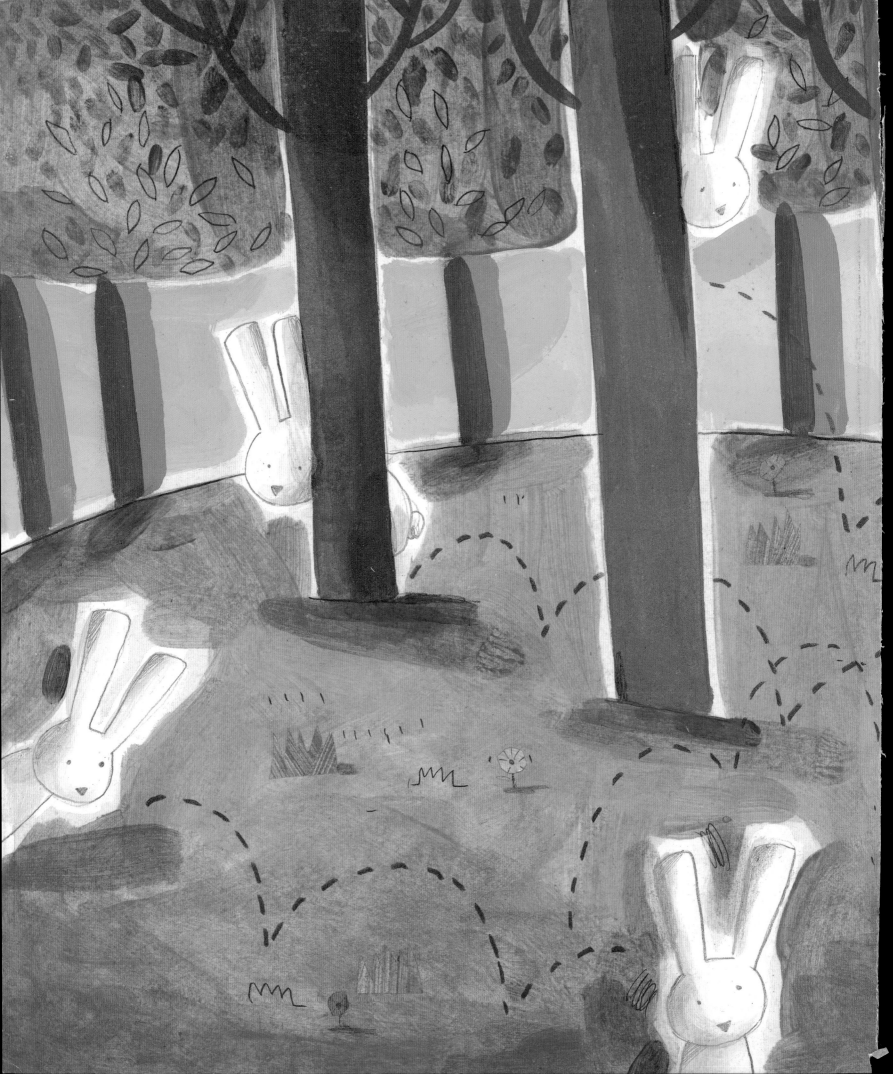